The Counterfeit Tackle

The Counterfeit Tackle

by Matt Christopher

Illustrated by Paul Casale

Little, Brown and Company

BOSTON   TORONTO   LONDON

Republished in 1990

ISBN 0-316-14243-3 (pb)

Library of Congress Catalog Card Number 65-17851

10 9 8 7 6 5 4 3 2

MV   NY

Published simultaneously in Canada
by Little, Brown & Company (Canada) Limited

PRINTED IN THE UNITED STATES OF AMERICA

To
Dominic

The Counterfeit Tackle

1

BUZZ stepped into the house and closed the door against the bitter cold air. His cheeks were apple-red. His glasses were clouding over so that he couldn't see a thing.

He put the sack of groceries on the table, took off his glasses and set them on the shelf beside the kitchen sink.

He turned and looked at his twin brother Corky. The two of them looked exactly alike except that Buzz was near-sighted and had to wear glasses.

3

"What's the matter, Corky?" Buzz asked. "Are you sick?"

Corky was sitting at the kitchen table, his chin cupped in his hands. If he wasn't sick, his thoughts were a million miles away. He mumbled something that sounded like "Yuh."

"Okay, keep it a secret," said Buzz. "I don't want to know your troubles, anyway."

He took off his cap and coat. It was Saturday, the last day of September, and it sure had gotten cold all of a sudden.

Dad appeared at the dining room door. His eyes met Buzz's. He didn't look especially well, either.

"Guess I'm to blame for this," he said. "I bought three tickets for the Bears-Giants game from Ben Welsh, thinking

4

that the three of us could go. But Corky feels he shouldn't go."

Buzz looked puzzledly from Dad to his brother. "Why not?"

"He thinks that if he doesn't show up at the Marlins game tomorrow, Coach Hayes will boot him off the team."

Buzz wrinkled his nose, a thing he always did whenever he heard something he didn't like. "Boot him off the team for that? I don't think Mr. Hayes would do that. Do you, Dad?"

Dad shrugged.

Corky lifted his face from his hands and shot piercing eyes at Buzz.

"Well, he would! You don't know Coach Hayes the way I do! He's tough. He doesn't want anybody to get there late or to miss a game. Just because I got there late last week he bawled me out.

6

He said that if I was late again I'd be benched. Imagine what he'd say if I didn't get there at all tomorrow!"

Corky played right tackle on the Otters football team. The season had opened last week and the Otters had beaten the Dolphins 21 to 19.

Buzz hadn't gone to the game. He had played basketball on his class team last year and was going to play again this year, but he didn't care for football. It seemed like just a lot of head-bashing to him.

Corky was different. He enjoyed football as well as basketball. He liked baseball, too. Buzz didn't. Buzz would rather swim and fish. And play chess. He was the school chess champion last year. That was a game he *really* liked.

"If I were you," he said to Corky, "I'd

go to the game, anyway. I just bet you that Coach Hayes won't boot you off the team."

"But you're not me," said Corky, and cupped his chin into his hands again. "And you don't know Coach Hayes."

Dad looked at Buzz. "How about you, Buzz? Will you go with me?"

Buzz lifted his shoulders and stuffed his hands into his pockets. "Sure. I'll go with you, Dad. But — " He paused.

"But what?"

"Well, Dougie was going to come over tomorrow. We were going to watch television for a while, then play chess. Wouldn't — wouldn't Mom and Joan care about going with you?"

Joan was their seventeen-year-old sister, who was a cheerleader in high

8

school. Certainly she might enjoy going to the Bears-Giants game.

Dad took a deep breath and let it out heavily. "Well, I don't know. If Corky plays tomorrow with the Otters, your mother probably would rather see him play. Maybe Joan will go with me."

He turned around just as Joan walked in from the other room. "Did I hear my name mentioned in vain?" she said, smiling.

"It all depends," said Dad. He explained about the tickets and the problem with Corky. Then he asked her if she'd like to go to the game.

Her brows shot up and her eyes opened wide. "Of course I'd like to go! And if neither of the twins wants to go, can I ask Steve to come along?"

Steve Post was her latest heartthrob. Two weeks ago it was Terry Slocum. Next week or two weeks from now it could be anybody's guess who her heartthrob would be.

"I suppose so," said Dad. "Buzz doesn't care about it, and Corky doesn't dare. I guess it'll be you, Steve and I, then."

All this went on and Corky never said a word. He just sat there with his chin in his hands and his eyes staring off into space.

Buzz knew that he wanted to go to that Giants-Bears game in the worst way. No one loved football as much as Corky did. He was crazy about those professional football games on television. Now that he had a chance to see a real big-league game in person, he couldn't. And just because he was afraid that Coach Hayes would kick him off the team.

Boy, thought Buzz. *I wouldn't be afraid. If I loved football the way Corky does,* I'd *go.*

This was the first time the two great teams had ever played in Kellsburg. It was a benefit game to raise money for a special fund. It might be the last time they would play here.

"Come on, Corky," said Dad. "There's a good game on television now. Let's watch it."

Later on Buzz put on his cap and coat again and went to the library. The wind was blowing hard and there were snow flurries in the air.

For several days Buzz had wanted to get a book or two on chess. He knew how to play the game fairly well, but not as well as he wished. The only person he hadn't beaten at school was Mr. Krum, his math teacher. And that was his aim — to beat the pants off Mr. Krum. Although, of course, he wouldn't tell it just that way to Mr. Krum.

He found two books on chess which he thought would help him. While he was waiting for Ms. Larkin, the librarian, to stamp his library card, a boy came up beside him.

"Buzz, is Corky home?"

It was Pete Nettles. He was smaller and younger than Buzz and a great buddy of Corky's, a thing Buzz couldn't understand. Pete was the dumbest kid on the block. He had just passed last year by the skin of his teeth. Yet Corky liked him.

"Yes, he's home," said Buzz in a not too friendly voice. "Why?"

Pete blinked a few times and stepped back a little. "I — I just wanted to see him, that's all."

"Well, you'd better not see him now," said Buzz. "He's too busy."

Pete's dark eyes hung on to his a moment. Then Pete turned away and headed for the shelves where a label read SPORTS.

Buzz smirked. *Sports. That kid would never be able to do anything.* Then he turned back and saw Ms. Larkin looking directly at him. It was a dark, unpleasant look — the kind Mom gave him when he acted smart at home — and his face turned a bright red.

"Guess I shouldn't have talked to him that way," he murmured quietly.

13

"No, Buzz," replied Ms. Larkin softly. "You shouldn't have."

Ms. Larkin placed his card in one of the books, then pushed them toward him.

"Thank you," he said. He picked up the books and left.

It was snowing harder now. The flakes were like pinfeathers whipping about in the air. They hit his glasses, melted, and left streaks. After a while they bothered him so that he had to take the glasses off.

"Hey, Corky, boy!" a voice shouted ahead of him. "Hope it stops snowing before our game tomorrow! Don't you?"

Buzz saw two boys approaching — Gary O'Brien and Tony Krebbs, members of the Otters football team. They stopped and smiled at him while the snow pelted their faces.

14

Buzz started to say something, but Gary was looking at the title of one of the books Buzz was carrying and he laughed.

"Hey, look at this, Tony! Corky's going to read up on chess! You don't expect to play chess like that smart brother of yours, do you, Cork?"

Buzz's heart skipped a beat. "I'm Buzz," he said. "I took my glasses off because of the snow." He pulled the glasses out of his pocket to prove it.

Gary's face colored. "Oh," he said. "Sorry, Buzz. Thought you were Corky. Come on, Tony. Let's go."

2

GARY and Tony brushed past Buzz and went on their way, and Buzz went on his. Both of those boys were in his class in school. But they often acted just that way, as if he had the measles or something.

They liked Corky. Everyone liked Corky. It wasn't because he played football, either. Or basketball. Buzz played basketball with some of those same guys. Still, it made no difference with them. They'd yell "Hi!" to Corky if they saw him half a mile away. But Buzz would practically have to bump into them before they said "Hi" to him. It wasn't the same kind of "Hi," either. It was dead-like.

Why they liked Corky and not him, Buzz didn't know. He had one friend — Dougie Byrd. One friend — as long as he was a *real* friend — was enough for him.

He got to thinking about tomorrow's pro football game. He sure wished Corky would go. It would be the greatest thing that ever happened to him. He'd remember it as long as he lived. Who knew if he'd ever have this chance again?

And then, suddenly, an idea popped into Buzz's head. A crazy, unbelievable, fantastic idea. But an idea that could work perfectly!

The more he thought about it, the better it looked, and the faster he hurried home.

He called Corky into the bedroom and shut the door. He was breathless with excitement.

"Corky, you still would like to go to the Giants-Bears game, wouldn't you?"

"Of course I would! But I told you —"

"Wait! I have an idea. You *can* go. And you won't have to worry about not playing with the Otters tomorrow, either!"

Corky stared. "Why? Did you talk with Coach Hayes?"

"No. I'll play in your place. Without my glasses on no one will know that I'm Buzz! I'll pretend I'm you!"

Corky's mouth dropped open. "That's crazy!"

18

"Sh-h!" whispered Buzz. "Not so loud! No one must know about this. Not even Dad. This is only between you and me."

"But you've only played football in gym!" Corky said, his voice just above a whisper. "How do you expect to do it?"

"Look, you play tackle, don't you? All you do is stand there in the line and try to keep the opponents from running through. What's hard about that?"

"Everything's hard about that," snapped Corky. "You have to stand just right. You have to know how to block your man. Buzz, you're not in condition! You could get hurt!"

"I played basketball all last winter just as much as you did," said Buzz. "And I rode my bike around this summer more often than you played baseball. You've only been practicing football a few weeks.

You can't be in much better condition than I am."

Corky took a deep breath. He stuck his hands into his pockets and turned around. He made a complete turn and looked squarely at Buzz again.

Now a faint smile was on his lips. He began to blink, as if he were ready to cry or something.

"What if someone catches on? I'll be kicked off the team and maybe the game will be forfeited."

"No one will catch on," said Buzz. "I'm sure of it. Just a little while ago Gary O'Brien and Tony Krebbs came up to me on the street and thought I was you! I had my glasses off because of the snow. They didn't know it was me until I told them."

Corky took a hand out of his pocket and rubbed it across his face.

"Don't you think we should tell Dad?" he asked.

"Dad wouldn't let us do it, Corky. He wouldn't go for anything like that. I know Dad. This has just got to be between you and me. When it's over with, no one will know the difference. There will be no harm done and you will have seen the Giants-Bears game."

Buzz got off the bed and looked directly into Corky's eyes. "Will you go and tell Dad you've changed your mind about seeing the Giants-Bears game, or do you want me to?"

"I — I think you'd better, Buzz," said Corky.

Buzz smiled. "Okay. I'll tell him."

They walked out of the room and

down the hall to the living room. Dad was sitting there, reading a hunting and fishing magazine. Buzz went up to him and told him that Corky had changed his mind. He'd decided he'd go to the Giants-Bears game.

Dad put his magazine down and smiled. "Well, fine. Did you have something to do with it, Buzz?"

Buzz nodded. "Yes. I talked to him. I convinced him that he ought to go."

"Good. You'll probably be a diplomat when you grow up. Now go and talk to your sister. It'll probably be disappointing news to her and to Steve."

Buzz shrugged. "I'll tell her," he said. "Maybe she hasn't called Steve yet."

But Joan had called Steve. She wasn't too disappointed at the news. She'd call Steve again, she said.

"Are you going to ask him to go on that third ticket?" said Buzz. "Or are you going?"

Joan's green eyes glimmered. "*I'm* going, of course."

After breakfast on Sunday morning, Buzz and Corky dressed in their oldest clothes and went out to the backyard. Buzz had his glasses off. It was cold but it wasn't snowing, nor was there snow on the ground.

Corky showed him how to get down in tackle position and how to throw a block.

"When you're out there you get in between Peter Monino and Gary O'Brien," said Corky. "Peter plays guard and Gary end. Get down like this and drive ahead with short, digging steps,"

24

he explained. "Never hold your man with your hands. Just block him from trying to get through. When the other team has the ball, you have to get through to tackle the ball-carrier. Drive your man out of the way with your shoulders. Like this."

Corky showed Buzz exactly what he meant.

They were out there for nearly fifteen minutes. Then Buzz realized that someone had walked into the yard and was standing nearby, watching them.

Buzz and Corky stopped and looked to see who it was. It was Pete Nettles, holding a Sunday newspaper in his hands. He was staring silently from Buzz to Corky, a very puzzled look on his face.

"Hi, Pete," Corky said, smiling. "Buzz and I are getting a little workout."

25

Pete's eyes lit up. "Hi, Corky! Who do you think is going to win today?"

"The Giants," said Corky, grinning. "I'll bet you a sundae."

Pete smiled. "I'll bet on the Bears," he said. "But I'm not talking about that game. I'm talking about the Otters game."

Buzz looked at Corky. Corky's face turned pink.

"Oh, we will, of course," said Corky. "Who do you think?"

"You'd better not bet on that one." Pete laughed. "It's against the law!"

3

DAD, Corky and Joan left for the Giants-Bears game immediately after lunch. Buzz could hardly wait for them to leave. The Otters-Marlins game began at one-thirty and he didn't want to be late. He *couldn't* be late.

He went into the bedroom and put on Corky's football uniform. It was brown with white trim and already had some smudges of dried mud on it. Number 76 was in great big print on both the front and back of the jersey.

27

He put on his own shoes and walked out of the room, carrying the football shoes and helmet in his hands.

He walked into the kitchen. His mother turned from the kitchen sink where she was doing the dishes. Her eyes went wide and Buzz thought that she was going to faint.

"Corky! I thought you — Why, you devil! You're Buzz! With that uniform on you had me fooled!" She wrung the suds off her hands and continued staring at him as if she couldn't believe what she saw.

"Just what do you think you're doing with that uniform on?" she cried, provoked. "You don't think for one minute that *you're* going to play in place of Corky, do you?"

"Please, Mom. Not so loud. Yes, I told

Corky I'd play in his place. You saw how anxious he was to see the Giants-Bears game, Mom."

"But this is ridiculous, Buzz," said Mom. "You just can't take Corky's place like that. Now go back into your bedroom and take off that uniform. Don't stall another second. Go on! Get!"

Buzz took a step backward. He started to choke up.

"Mom," he pleaded, "please let me do this. I promised Corky. We look so much alike it's as if we are one person, anyway. Even you didn't recognize me right away. It's not that I'm going to commit a crime, Mom."

She looked at him for a long while. Gradually, the anger faded from her eyes and face.

She took a deep breath and let it out slowly. "You didn't tell your father about this, did you?"

"No. But I'll tell him — afterwards," Buzz said seriously.

"You know," Mom said, looking directly into Buzz's eyes, "you might be very sorry about this."

"You make it sound as if I'm going to rob a bank or something, Mom." He went up to her. "Please, I've got to do it now. I promised Corky."

She looked straight into his eyes. She was a lot taller than he was, and her eyes were dark and shiny. She was quiet a long while, thinking.

"All right," she said at last. "I suppose it's too late to do anything now. I hope for your sake — and Corky's — that everything goes all right. But if it doesn't — " She shook her head, and her eyes were hard as she looked at him.

A big smile splashed across Buzz's face. "Thanks, Mom!" he said happily. He kissed her on the cheek and rushed out of the door.

He walked about half a block when a car pulled to the curb across the street and its horn tooted.

"Hey, Corky! Come on!"

Buzz saw that it was Mr. Marsh in his green station wagon. His son Goose was with him. His name was Jerry but everybody called him Goose because of his long, skinny neck. Other kids on the Otters football team were in the car, too.

Buzz felt a funny sensation in the pit of his stomach as he started across the street. Here was another test, he thought. Would Mr. Marsh recognize him? Would Goose or any of the others notice that he wasn't Corky, but Buzz?

Every time he met someone new it was a test.

He climbed into the car and forced a grin. "Hi, Mr. Marsh," he said. "Hi, gang."

"Hello, Corky, old boy!" cried Goose, showing one missing tooth as he smiled. "How come you're walking? You want to be late again?"

"I couldn't help it," said Buzz. The butterflies were fluttering like mad in his stomach. "Mom — well, she wanted to see me about some things before I left. I can't take a chance on being late again."

"I guess not!" Tony Krebbs chuckled. "Not unless you want to sit on the bench!"

33

The butterflies stopped fluttering. Well, most of them did, anyway. Everyone in the car thought he was Corky. If he fooled them, he should be able to fool all the other members of the team, too.

They arrived at the football field. Mr. Marsh parked the station wagon in the parking lot and the boys piled out. They walked to the benches that were lined up two or three yards in front of the bleachers, took off their regular shoes and put on their football shoes.

Coach Hayes walked by with a couple of footballs in his arms.

"Well, see you made it in time today," he said to Buzz. A wide grin was on his sun-tanned, ruddy face.

Buzz smiled. "Yes, sir, I did," he said.

He stood up and the coach tossed him a football. "Here. Find someone to play

34

catch with. Then you, Foote and the other linemen better get together and go through a few drills."

Buzz caught the football and trotted out with it onto the field. The Marlins, in their green and white uniforms, were at the other end of the field. The Otters were warming up on this end.

Buzz played catch with Michael Foote and Goose Marsh. Both boys were running around and Buzz had trouble throwing to them. He couldn't get a grip on the ball and realized that that was one thing that he and Corky had not talked about. He held the ball in his hand loosely and heaved it the best he could. The ball wobbled and rose high into the air but never went more than twelve or fifteen yards.

He had trouble without his glasses,

too. He could see things up close pretty well, but objects in the distance looked fuzzy.

Boy, he'd be lucky to get through this.

Soon other members of the team ran out upon the field, including Craig Smith, Jimmy Briggs, Alan Rogers and Frosty Homan. Buzz soon discovered that they were the backfield men.

"Okay, let's run through some drills," snapped Craig.

The boys quickly hurried into their positions. All except Buzz. He trotted around, pretending he was limbering up his legs. Actually he was just waiting to see where he was supposed to go.

"Corky, what are you waiting for?" snapped Craig.

"Who? Me?" said Buzz. "Nothing!"

He saw an open space between Peter

Monino and Gary O'Brien. He hurried to fill it, remembering that Corky had told him that his right tackle position was between Pete and Gary.

"Okay. Get set! One! Two! Three! Hike!"

At the word "Hike!" the line charged forward. Every man moved at the same time, except Buzz. He was a fraction of a second late.

"Corky, you're dragging! Snap into it!" said Craig.

They tried it again. Now Buzz was ready. At the word "Hike!" he sprang forward at the same time the others did.

After a while Craig said, "Okay. That'll be enough. Pass the footballs around a while."

They started running around the field, passing and catching.

"Corky, take off!" shouted a voice.

Buzz saw that it was Goose Marsh. He was ready to throw a football. Buzz started to run. Goose heaved the ball. It spiraled through the air in a high arc, not wobbling a bit.

For a moment the ball looked blurry, then cleared as it got closer. Buzz caught it on the run, stopped, heaved it back. It was a poor throw. *I'll never be able to throw a football,* he thought.

Goose picked it up after it bounced around a bit, then threw Buzz another long pass.

The ball sailed over Buzz's head and bounced toward the sideline. There were people standing several feet behind it, waiting for the game to begin.

The ball rolled across the white line before Buzz could pick it up. As he rose with it he came almost face to face with someone he knew very well. Dougie Byrd, his best friend!

Buzz grinned. "Hi, Dougie!" he said. "Coming over tonight to play chess?"

Dougie stared at him. Then Buzz turned away quickly, his face beet red.

He had forgotten he was supposed to be Corky, not Buzz!

4

"I THOUGHT you didn't like chess,
Corky!" said Dougie.

Buzz turned and forced a smile. His
neck was burning. "I don't," he said.
"But Buzz brought some books about
chess home yesterday and I read them.
Oh — forget it, Dougie!"

Buzz ran off, trying to put a lot of distance between him and Dougie before
Dougie could say anything more to him.
Some of the fans started to chuckle
behind him. They certainly must have

gotten a kick out of listening to that silly conversation about chess.

A few moments later the whistle shrilled and the football field cleared. Buzz trotted to the Otters' bench where the entire team was standing, facing Coach Hayes. Buzz felt an arm rest on one shoulder, than an arm rest on the other shoulder. He looked at the guys on either side of him. They were Goose Marsh and Frosty Homan.

Something warm and good went through him as those arms rested on his shoulders.

Coach Hayes named off the starting lineup. Corky's name was included. A whistle shrilled and Buzz saw the three referees standing at the middle of the field.

"Okay, let's get out there!" said Coach Hayes. "The old hustle!"

41

Both teams ran out onto the field. Quarterback Craig Smith and left halfback Jimmy Briggs headed for the referees, as did two men from the Marlins team. Craig, Buzz had learned, was captain. Jimmy was co-captain.

The coin was tossed. Craig called it. He must have won. "We'll receive," Buzz heard him say.

The Marlins chose the north goal. A moment later both teams were ready. The referee lifted his hand, blew his whistle, and the Marlins kicked off.

The kick was shallow. The ball hardly spun as it shot through the air. Jimmy caught it against his stomach and started to run forward with it. Buzz was already running down the field, looking for a man to block. The whole Marlins team was charging forward like an army. All eleven men had their sights on Jimmy.

Buzz got in front of a Marlin man, lifted his arms to block him. He let out a grunt as the man pushed him aside. He fell to one knee, rose, plunged ahead to block another man.

The whistle shrilled. Jimmy had been tackled. Buzz's heart pounded as the Otters gathered into a huddle.

"Forty-three," said Craig. "Corky! Pete! Break open that hole!"

They broke out of the huddle, went into a T formation. The ball was on the twenty-seven-yard line. It was first and ten.

"Ready! One! Two! Three! Hike!"

Tony Krebbs centered the ball. Craig caught it, spun halfway around, shoved

43

the ball against Frosty's stomach. The fullback put both arms around it and plunged through right tackle. Buzz tried to shove his man aside. He felt himself thrust backward instead. He caught a glimpse of Frosty plunging past him, then Frosty being pulled down by the Marlins' big tackle.

A yard loss.

"Corky!" Coach Hayes shouted from the sideline. "Keep your shoulders down! Down!"

On the next play Buzz kept his shoulders down. He dug his toes into the hard ground, too, remembering what Corky had told him.

This time Craig threw a screen pass. He was well protected by his linemen as he flipped the short, spiraling pass to Jimmy Briggs. Jimmy caught it and ran toward the left side of the field, dodged a couple of Marlin tacklers, then was knocked out of bounds on the thirty-eight-yard line. A twelve-yard gain!

"Nice run, Jimmy!" said Craig.

"Nice pass!" smiled Jimmy.

In the next play the Otters got the ball across the forty-yard line, the midway mark on the eighty-yard-long field. In three downs they moved it to the Marlins' eighteen.

Beads of sweat lay on Buzz's forehead. He took back everything he had said about the tackle position's being easy. There was more to it than just crouching there and staring into your opponent's eyes. Blocking him and driving forward to open up a hole for your ball carrier were acts that took a lot of energy. This was no job for a weak kid.

45

Buzz began to realize that he wasn't as strong as he had thought. It was a good thing that there were ten other men on the team who were in better condition than he was.

Right halfback Alan Rogers caught a short pass that netted another four yards, putting the Otters on the Marlins' fourteen. On the next play Craig faked a pass, then handed the ball off to Frosty.

Frosty fumbled it! He tried to pick it up and accidentally kicked it. Marlin men charged through the line and a mad scramble for the ball followed.

Someone fell on it. There was a pile-up of green and brown uniforms that looked like a quickly made-up sandwich. The whistle shrilled, and one by one the players unpiled.

Buzz look anxiously to see who was at

the bottom. Whoever it was must be flattened out like a pancake.

It was Frosty. By a miracle, he wasn't flattened at all. Under his chin was the football, with his arms wrapped tightly around it.

It was an eight-yard loss. Buzz glanced around at some of the Otters' faces around him. They all looked as if they'd eaten green apples.

Third down. Fourteen yards to go for a first down. The ball was on the Marlins' twenty-two-yard line.

Craig passed. It was long and spiraling beautifully! Reaching up his hands near the end zone was Goose Marsh! He caught it, and was tackled almost in the same spot.

Three yards from the goal line!

"We want a touchdown! We want a

touchdown!" yelled a host of Otter fans from the sideline.

First and goal to go.

Frosty took the hand-off from Craig and bucked the line. One-yard gain.

He tried it again.

No gain. Third down. Two yards to go.

In the huddle Buzz looked squarely at Craig. "Have Frosty take it between me and Pete. We'll open a hole for him big enough for a truck."

Craig looked back at him. "Okay, Corky. We'll try it. We've *got* to get this touchdown!"

They broke out of the huddle. The teams lined up, facing each other at the line of scrimmage. Craig began barking signals. The ball was snapped. Craig took it, turned, handed off to Frosty. Frosty charged into the line between right

guard and right tackle, where Pete Monino and Buzz were digging their toes into
the turf, driving back their opponents.

The hole was there. Maybe it wasn't
big enough for a truck, but it was big
enough for Frosty. He went through it
and over the goal line.

A touchdown!

Frosty kicked for the extra point but
missed by inches. The Otters went into
the lead, 6 to 0.

Craig and Goose ran up beside Buzz,
smiling happily.

"Thataway, Corky! You and Pete sure
opened up a hole that time!"

Buzz was panting from all that hard
work. It was almost too much of an effort
to smile. But he smiled, anyway. It was
what Corky would do.

It was what he wanted to do, too.

50

5

THE Marlins ran the kickoff back to the Otters' twenty-four-yard line. On the very first play Ollie Colt, the Marlins' speedy fullback, busted through left tackle for a sixteen-yard gain. Buzz found himself lying flat on his back. He didn't even know what had hit him.

With goal to go the Marlins tried a pass. Craig intercepted it! He ran it back to his eleven, where he was tackled hard.

Two plays later the first quarter ended.

Substitutions came in for Buzz and a couple of other players.

"Nice hole you made there for Frosty," Coach Hayes complimented Buzz. "But what happened to you in that other play, Corky? When Ollie Colt went on that long run. Do you know?"

"No, I don't," said Buzz. "I was trying to bust through to get after him. The next thing I knew somebody knocked me on my tail."

"Right. And that was because you weren't crouched down. You had your shoulders and your head up. I haven't seen you do that before. At least not this year."

"Guess I just forgot," said Buzz, trying to avoid the coach's eyes.

If he slipped up in some way now, and the coach realized he wasn't Corky but Buzz, he'd certainly be in a fix. Corky would be in a worse fix. He'd be kicked off the team for sure.

The coach patted Buzz's knee. "Just remember to keep those shoulders down. You have to keep your head up a little to look the other guy in the eye. But don't stand up so that he could knock you off balance. You're no good in there then."

Buzz nodded.

When the referee announced that there were four minutes left before the first half was over, Coach Hayes sent Buzz back into the game. The Otters had the ball on their thirty-two-yard line.

They lost a yard on a line plunge, but gained it back on a quick pass over center. Craig passed again on the third down. This time they lacked a yard for a first down.

In the huddle Craig looked at Buzz. Buzz knew what ran through the captain's mind. Craig was remembering that touchdown they had gotten and that it was Buzz who was mostly responsible.

A smile flashed across Craig's face. "Can you and Pete open up another big hole, Corky?"

Buzz looked at Pete and smiled back. "Sure, if Frosty can hang on to that ball without fumbling it."

As soon as he said that, he looked at Frosty Homan. Frosty's eyes lowered and his face colored.

That was a wrong thing to say! I knew it! Corky would never have said that! Not to Frosty, one of the most quiet, bashful kids around.

"Okay. Let's go," said Craig, slapping his hands together.

Buzz and Pete made the hole and Frosty plowed through for a five-yard gain. As they headed back across the line of scrimmage, Buzz looked aside at Frosty. Frosty met his eye briefly, then looked away.

I can't let him be mad, thought Buzz. *I know that Corky likes him.*

He walked up beside Frosty. "Frosty," he said softly, "I'm sorry about that crack I made. I didn't mean it."

Frosty shrugged. "Forget it."

"You made a nice run just now," added Buzz. "You can really move, Frosty."

Frosty looked up and smiled. "Thanks, Corky. But if you and Pete hadn't opened up that hole, I wouldn't have been able to do it. You guys deserve credit, too."

"Oh, well," grinned Buzz. "I suppose it's in the line of duty!"

With a minute and a half to go before the half ended, Craig tossed a lateral to Jimmy Briggs. Jimmy then heaved a pass to Gary, who was running down toward the right sideline.

Suddenly a Marlin backfield man bolted out in front of Gary, intercepted the pass, and raced all the way down the sideline for a touchdown!

They converted for the extra point, made it, and the score was Marlins 7, Otters 6.

Buzz trotted up alongside Goose Marsh. "They struck like lightning that time, didn't they?"

Goose shook his head unhappily. "It takes one bad play," he said. "*Phoot!* and you're behind."

Craig ran the kickoff back to the Marlins' thirty-three. Jimmy gained four yards on an end-around play, then Craig tried a screen pass to Alan Rogers. It was high and wobbly, definitely the worst pass Craig had ever thrown.

Alan leaped high for it. He caught the ball, but he couldn't hang on to it. At that moment Buzz, who had learned earlier what to do on a screen-pass play, was standing behind the line of scrimmage. He was blocking his man from trying to get at the passer.

Then his man broke past him. It was then that he saw Alan, who was only a few feet away from him, leap high for the pass.

When Alan fumbled the ball it bounced against his knee, struck the defender's shoulder and landed in Buzz's hands. Stunned, Buzz could think of nothing but to run with it. He started running along the thirty-yard stripe until the field was clear ahead, then turned sharply toward the Marlins' goal, and the goal posts that were fuzzy images in the distance.

"Run, Corky! Run!" a voice shouted. Other voices joined in.

He crossed the twenty-five, the twenty, the fifteen. To his left he saw the Marlin safety man gaining ground fast. Buzz tried to step up his speed. If he did, it wasn't enough. He was hit on the nine-yard line and went down. When he crawled to his feet, the referee spotted the ball on the seven.

Goose, Craig — the whole Otters team — pounded him happily on the back.

"Nice running, Corky!"

"Man, I never saw you move so fast before in my life!"

"Terrific, Corky!"

Craig put an arm around his neck. "You saved my life, buddy! That ball slipped out of my hand!"

"Just lucky that the Marlin guy didn't catch it and that I was there," smiled Buzz.

"If you had caught that ball before it had hit that Marlin guy, you couldn't have run," said Craig. "It would've been an incompleted pass."

Buzz stared. Boy, football certainly had the strangest rules!

Frosty bucked the line for a two-yard gain, then Craig pushed forward for another two. The Marlin line held like a wall, giving just a little.

With third down and three yards to go

for a touchdown, Craig turned anxious eyes to Buzz and Pete in the huddle. Buzz knew what he was thinking. Break open a hole for Frosty.

Buzz smiled. "Pete and I are ready, Captain," he said.

Craig grinned. "Good! Okay, Frosty! Get on your horse!"

This time things were different. The hole was there one moment and closed the next. A Marlin linebacker had plugged it.

When the pile-up was unscrambled the ball was on the one-yard line. Last down. One yard to go. And only seconds before the end of the half.

"This has to be it!" said Craig through tightly clenched teeth. "Frosty, run it through *left* tackle this time. The change might fool them just enough."

61

They went into their regular T formation. Craig barked signals. The ball was snapped. Craig took it, handed off to Frosty. Frosty bolted through left tackle.

It seemed that every Marlin linebacker was there helping their linemen plug every hole and keep them from giving an inch. When the whistle blew it was hard to tell whether Frosty had made it or not. It was very close.

He didn't make it! There was still a foot to go!

The ball went to the Marlins. They had time for one play. Then the half ended.

Goose trotted up beside Buzz as the teams walked off the field.

"Come over after the game, Corky," Goose invited. "My mother's making those cookies you like so much. She asked me to ask you."

Buzz looked curiously at Goose. Corky had never said anything about eating cookies at Goose's place. But then, Corky hardly talked to him about his friends. That was all right, because Buzz never cared to listen, anyway. They were Corky's friends, not his. Why should he care what Corky and his friends did?

He weighed Goose's invitation with interest. The Marlins-Otters game would get over long before the Giants-Bears game. He'd have plenty of time to go over to Goose's house before Dad and Corky returned home. He'd sure like to try some of Mrs. Marsh's cookies.

"Okay, Goose," he said. "I'll come over."

6

THE second half started. The Marlins began to move down the field like a steamroller. Twice they tried long forward passes, but each time the ball was batted down. It was their short passes, and their runs, that clicked for yardage.

They lost ground when twice they were penalized five yards for being off-side. They were on the Otters' eight-yard line when they committed another foul.

This time it was a severe one. Fifteen yards for tripping!

The Marlins called for time-out. The Otters didn't mind. They were happy to have a chance to breathe freely awhile, too.

Buzz saw Craig, Frosty, and some of the others watching the Marlins like hawks, as if trying to see what strategy they were going to pull off next. So far the penalties had not bothered the Marlins very much. They had only slowed the Marlins' forward drives. They had not stopped them.

Time was up. Once more the Marlins pressed forward.

On the third down their quarterback faked a hand-off to Ollie Colt, then faded back to pass. He flipped a fast one to his right end which Jimmy Briggs tried to reach but couldn't. The end caught it, crossed the goal line, and the Marlins had another touchdown.

Ollie Colt booted the extra point and the score was Marlins 14, Otters 6.

Buzz saw Craig's face as the Otters team turned and walked down the field. His unhappy look explained how much this game meant to Craig.

He looked at the other players and saw the same expression on their faces. He knew how they felt. He had felt that way many times while playing basketball.

Now he began to feel that way, too. He felt sorry for Craig and Frosty and the whole Otters team. Corky had told him that the Otters had lost their first game to the Dolphins. So of course they wanted badly to win this one.

It was a short season. They played only six games. They *needed* to win this one, or perhaps they would lose all their confidence and not win another game this year.

"Come on, you guys!" yelled Buzz. He had often been the one to stimulate the basketball players when they felt this way. "Let's buckle down and do something! We're far from being beat!"

Craig looked at him. Then Jimmy, and Goose, and the others looked at him.

The discouraged look vanished from Craig's face and was replaced by one of enthusiasm.

"Come on!" he shouted. "They're only eight points ahead! Let's go!"

They got into position to receive the kickoff. Ollie Colt kicked off for the Marlins. It was high and about ten yards in from the out-of-bounds line. Alan took it and ran it back to the twenty-nine.

Two line plunges didn't get him any-where. A pass to Jimmy netted eight yards. Then Craig gained a first down on the quarterback sneak.

They tried a pass again. This time it was knocked down. Again Craig called for a pass, handing off to Frosty Homan to make the throw. Frosty faded back and passed to right end Gary O'Brien.

Gary made a beautiful catch, but he was across the out-of-bounds line when he caught the ball. The pass was declared incomplete.

Then a pass to Goose succeeded for an eleven-yard gain.

The boys grinned happily as they ran back into a huddle. "Now we're going," said Goose.

They tried a different play. Craig faded back, faked a pass to Goose, then tossed a pitch-out to Alan Rogers.

Alan fumbled the ball! A Marlin guard picked it up and started running with it down the field!

Buzz went after him. The Marlin player was about his size and not any faster. Buzz caught up with him, wrapped his arms around the player's waist and brought him down.

"Nice tackle, Corky!" cried Gary.

"Thanks," said Buzz. "But they've got the ball now. Not us."

The referee brought the ball in to the in-bounds line and spotted it on the Marlins' thirty-two. On the very next play Buzz was knocked backwards on his tail, leaving a hole for the Marlin ball-carrier.

Angrily, Buzz sprang to his feet and rushed after a Marlin guard who was ready to throw a block on an Otter player. He threw himself alongside the man for a perfect block and the Otter man — who turned out to be Alan — pulled down the runner in a nifty tackle.

Buzz rose to his feet with satisfaction. He had let himself be caught off guard on the line, but that block had helped a lot in stopping the runner from making a long run. Possibly even from making a touchdown.

Then he saw a red flag on the ground less than two yards away. The referee came running forward. He pointed at Buzz.

"Clipping!" he said, and made chopping motions against the back of his leg. The clipping sign.

Buzz stared, his heart sinking to his knees. There were certainly some crazy rules in football!

The referee discussed the charge with the Marlin captain. The Marlins could take either the gain the runner had made — which was six yards — with the down counting, or take the fifteen yards with the down not counting. The Marlin captain accepted the fifteen yards with the down not counting.

Then a storm of insults flew through the air — all directed at Buzz!

"Corky! You crazy nut!" Craig looked at him with wide, shocked eyes. "You know you can't throw a block on a guy from behind!"

"Criminies, Cork!" said Goose, looking

as amazed as if Buzz had just pulled the most foolish play of the season. Which he undoubtedly had. "You know better than that!"

7

BUZZ could say nothing. He couldn't tell Craig or Goose that he had never heard of clipping before. At least, not in football. This was the first time he knew that a player couldn't throw a block from the rear. Corky hadn't said anything about that to him. But, of course, Corky couldn't tell him everything in that short space of time.

The Otters held the Marlins for two plays before the quarter ended.

To start the fourth quarter, the Marlins

threw a long pass to their right end. It proved to be one of their very few mistakes of the game. Goose swept in and intercepted the pass.

His legs looked like bicycle spokes winking in the sunlight as he ran down the field. The whole Marlins team was after him, but none ever got close enough to stop him.

He crossed the goal line for a touchdown.

The Otter fans cheered and yelled. Every man on the team slapped Goose happily on the back.

Frosty missed the extra point by kicking the ball a foot outside of the uprights. The score: Marlins 14, Otters 12.

The Otters kicked off, and for a while the Marlins were unable to move as swiftly as they had during the first half.

They were probably bewildered by that interception that had resulted in a touchdown. And they were probably tired. Whatever was troubling them was showing now in the way they played.

They lost the ball to the Otters on the Otters' thirty-six. The Otters made two plays, taking them across midfield to the Marlins' thirty-eight. Then the referee blew his whistle and announced that there were four minutes left in the game.

A pass failed to click, so the Otters punted to get the ball as close to the Marlins' goal line as possible.

The Marlins worked it back to their thirty-one. On the fourth down they punted. Buzz knew what they were doing. As long as they kept the football in Otter territory or, at least, far enough away from the Marlins' end zone, the

Otters would have little chance of scoring. The Marlins had a two-point lead. All they were interested in was letting the time run out.

Frosty caught the punt and ran it back to his twenty-two. They gained a first down on a pass to Jimmy, then another first down on a drive through right tackle.

Two of the four minutes were up. The ball was on the Marlins' thirty-six. The Otters inched forward, lost five yards on an off-side penalty charge, and found themselves a long way from the goal line with time running out fast.

Craig called for a double-reverse. They had only tried it once, during the first half. He handed off to Jimmy. Jimmy started running, then handed off to Alan. Alan swept around left end and, getting a key block from Frosty, dashed all the way down the field for a touch-down!

This time Frosty made the extra point.

Forty seconds later the game was over. The Otters had won, 19 to 14.

"What a game!" said Goose as he walked off the field with Buzz. "I didn't think we'd pull that one out."

Buzz smiled. "That double-reverse is neat. Why doesn't Craig call for it more often?"

"It isn't smart to call for some plays too often," explained Goose. "The other team will catch on, and then you haven't got anything left to surprise them with."

"Oh," said Buzz. "Guess that is smart."

Goose stared bewilderedly at him. "You all right, Corky?"

Buzz looked at him. "Of course I'm all right. Why?"

"Well, you just sounded as if you never heard of a double-reverse before."

Buzz's neck reddened. "Are you kidding?" he said. He groped for a better excuse so that Goose wouldn't get suspicious of him. "I just wondered why Craig didn't call the play more often, that's all. Hey, look who's coming."

Pete Nettles had broken away from the crowd at the sideline and was running over the field toward him. A wide grin was on his face as if it were his hero who had pulled the last, spectacular play that had won the game.

"Hi, Corky! Hi, Goose!"

Buzz grinned. "Hi, Pete. How did you like the game?"

Pete's coming was a lifesaver. Pete,

Goose and Corky were like the Three Musketeers — they were together most of the time. If Goose had started to get suspicious at all, Pete's presence made him forget it completely.

"It was sure close," said Pete. "Good thing Goose was there to intercept that pass. Nice work, Goose."

"Thanks, Pete," said Goose.

They reached the edge of the field. Waiting for them were Pete's parents.

"Hello, boys," greeted Mr. Nettles. "Nice interception, Goose. That play was the shot in the arm the boys needed."

"Thanks, Mr. Nettles." Goose smiled modestly.

"See you changed your mind about going to that Giants-Bears game, Corky," said Mr. Nettles, smiling. "It must have been at the last minute, because that's

80

where your dad said you two, and your sister, were heading when I saw you."

For the second time within the last two minutes Buzz's neck turned hot as fire. "Yes, I did," he said. "I . . . changed my mind at the last minute. Buzz went instead. I . . . thought that playing here was more important."

"Boy, that took a lot of gumption," said Mr. Nettles. "There're a lot of kids who'd like to see that pro game. Matter of fact, I would, too. But the tickets were all sold out by the time I wanted to buy any. Well, see you later, boys. Let's go, Pete."

8

"WELL, my great impersonator," Mom said as Buzz closed the kitchen door behind him, "I see you're still in one piece."

Buzz dropped the football helmet and shoes on the floor and began to pull off his jersey.

"I'm not too sure if I am," he said. "Wait'll I take off all this equipment. Maybe it's holding me together."

After he had the jersey and shoulder

pads off he was pretty well sure that he was really in one piece. He carried the stuff into his bedroom, finished undressing, then carried his clean clothes into the bathroom.

"Did anyone get suspicious about you?" Mom's voice carried to him from the kitchen.

A proud smile flicked across Buzz's face. "Not a bit, Mom. There were a few times when I did things and said things that almost put me in hot water for a minute, though. Sometimes I forgot what Corky had told me about crouching in the line, and Coach Hayes bawled me out. Well — not really, but he said he had never seen me in line with my head and shoulders up like that before."

Mom laughed. "And, of course, he

83

never had," she said. "Buzz, I've never seen the likes of you in my life. Take your bath and get dressed. By the way, was Pete Nettles at the game?"

"I'll say he was. So were his mother and father. You don't think he'd miss seeing Corky play, do you? Or Goose?"

"That's what I thought," said Mom. "So don't be surprised if Pete shows up and wants you to go out with him."

"Oh, no!" cried Buzz. "If he finds out I wasn't Corky he'll broadcast it to every kid in the neighborhood. Me and Corky both will be in *steaming* hot water then!"

"Don't worry about Pete," Mom said reassuringly. "He likes Corky too much to tell on him like that. Take your bath. We can talk later."

After a warm, refreshing bath he dried himself, dressed and combed his hair.

He remembered what Mom had said about the strong possibility of Pete's coming over, and wished Dad and Corky were home. But they weren't, and he had no idea when they would be.

Then he thought of something that had popped into his mind every once in a while during the game. Never before in his entire life had so many guys been so friendly toward him. And it was all because of one thing: they thought he was Corky.

He thought back to the basketball games in which he had played. Not even in them had the players been friendly toward him. Of course they had not been *un*friendly. But none of them had ever gone out of the way to slap him on the back or say nice words to him as the players had during the football game today. It made him feel . . . well, real good inside.

They weren't bad guys at all. They didn't act anything like they usually did when they saw him on the street. They acted . . . well, different. Almost as if they weren't the same kids.

He tried to explain some of this to his mother. "I know Corky and I are different in certain ways, Mom," he said, after he had given her a few examples of what had happened. "But we can't be that different, could we? Not if we look so much alike that nobody can tell us apart."

His mother looked at him silently. There was just a flicker of a smile on her lips.

"You do look almost exactly alike," she agreed. "But inside, you are made up of different stuff. This stuff is what gives

86

you a certain personality. It's this personality that comes out of you when you do things, when you say things, or when you meet people. It's this stuff inside of you two boys that makes you different from each other. It's like two houses that look exactly alike but have different families in them."

Buzz weighed her words. He nodded silently. "I'm getting the idea, Mom," he said softly.

The jangling phone interrupted them. Buzz answered it.

"Corky?" a voice asked.

Buzz reflected on the name for a second. The voice sounded like Goose Marsh's.

He couldn't say that Corky wasn't home. As far as Goose knew, Corky had played football today and must be home.

"Yes, this is Corky," said Buzz.

"Coming over?"

Suddenly Buzz remembered Goose Marsh's invitation to go over to his house for some of those cookies Corky was supposed to love so much.

"Oh, that's right," he said. "I almost forgot. I'll be over in a little while, Goose."

"Okay. I'll see you, Cork."

"That was Goose Marsh," Buzz said to his mother. "He invited me over for some cookies. He said that his mother had baked some of the ones Corky was so crazy about."

His mother's brows arched a little. "Oh?" she said. Then a smile brushed across her lips and she turned back to her work. She was mixing up a salad for the evening's supper. Buzz suspected that Mom was getting a kick out of something.

"What're you smiling like that for, Mom?" he asked.

"Those cookies," Mom confessed. Now she couldn't contain herself from breaking out in a laugh. "If it's the kind Corky's crazy about, they're raisin cookies!"

"Raisin? Oh, no!" cried Buzz, and dropped helplessly into a chair. "I hope they're not raisin!"

But they were. Mrs. Marsh had made a whole panful of them. Her blue eyes twinkled merrily as she offered the cookies to Buzz.

"Take several, Corky," she said. "They're free."

Buzz took one. "One's enough. Thanks, Mrs. Marsh."

"Oh, now, Corky. What's come over you? Why, you've never settled for less than four or five. Come on. Take some more."

Buzz looked up at Mrs. Marsh's twinkling eyes, then reached up and took another one. "Thanks, Mrs. Marsh. Maybe I'll have another after I finish these."

"Of course, you will," she said. She put the plate on the dining room table and covered it. "Well, Jerry said that you boys had a close game today."

"We sure did," said Buzz, and bit into the raisin cookie. He tried all he could not to show a face, because this raisin cookie tasted exactly the way he thought it would. Horrible.

"Did I sweeten it too much?" asked

Mrs. Marsh, the smile fading momentarily from her lips.

"No. I think it's just right," said Buzz.

"Well, I thought you squinched a little," said Mrs. Marsh. "It could be a little sweeter than usual. Wait. I'll bring you a glass of milk. You'll want something to wash it down with, anyway."

"Oh, you needn't bring me milk, Mrs. Marsh," protested Buzz.

Almost in the same breath he wanted to add, *But please do. Anything to wash away the horrible taste of these raisins!*

He didn't know how he managed to eat four raisin cookies. It was a good thing that Mrs. Marsh had offered him milk. Buzz thanked God for cows.

He left soon afterward, two cookies wrapped up in a piece of wax paper stuck inside his pocket. "Two for the road," Mrs. Marsh had said they were.

Buzz had a better idea. *Two for Corky,* he thought to himself.

He was halfway home when he met Pete coming down the street.

"Hi, Corky," greeted Pete. "Stopped at your house, but you weren't home."

"Naturally," said Buzz. The remark came out gruffly, as if Buzz had spoken, not Corky. He quickly smiled. Pete was kind of on the dumb side, but so what? Everyone couldn't be blessed with a lot of brains. "Where are you going, Pete?"

A happy smile crossed Pete's face. "How'd you like to have an ice cream sundae? Or a soda?"

Buzz stared. "You mean you'll . . . treat?"

"'Course!"

"Well . . ." Buzz laughed. "Why not?"

It just proved how much Pete liked Corky. And I bet that Corky's treated him lots of times, too, thought Buzz. I'm sure learning things. Not only about Corky, but myself, too.

They entered the soda shop on the corner. Buzz ordered a vanilla ice cream soda and Pete ordered the same. Pete got to talking about the football game, and now and then Buzz put in a few words.

Something must be wrong with me, thought Buzz. *I think I'm enjoying his company.*

Someone came into the shop and plunked himself on the seat beside Buzz. It was Frosty Homan. With him was Tony Krebbs.

94

"Hello, guys," greeted Frosty. "We're just heading for the Tower. Why don't you come with us?"

"I'll go with you!" cried Pete.

"Okay. How about you, Corky?"

The Tower?

He had never been up in the Tower. It was the last place in the world he'd ever want to go!

9

I DON'T know," Buzz said. "I'd better get home. We're having supper soon."

"Supper?" said Tony. "In the middle of the afternoon?"

Tony was exaggerating. But Buzz realized that it really wasn't as late as he'd thought.

"Come on, Corky," insisted Pete. "We haven't been up in the Tower in a long time."

Buzz knew that Corky had been up in the Tower at least a dozen times. He'd probably accept this invitation without hesitating a minute. In that case Buzz had better not offer any more excuses to get out of it or maybe one of the guys would get suspicious.

"Wait'll I finish this soda," he said.

He finished it in a couple of gulps, then spun on the stool and got off.

What if Dad, Corky, and Joan are driving down the street while we're walking? he thought, as all four of the boys headed for the Tower. *Our goose will surely be cooked then.*

I should have given my glasses to Corky. All he'd have to do is put them on the moment he saw someone he knew. That would have solved everything. What a time to think of that now!

The Tower was located on a side street outside of town. It was situated on a hill and was about one hundred feet high. It was an old observation tower which had once been used to spot airplanes for civil defense. The paint on the cabin was nearly all peeled off now and the windows were broken.

Pete was the first to reach the steel ladder. He climbed it to the first narrow platform about twenty feet up, then started up the next ladder. After him went Tony, then Frosty, then . . . Buzz wanted to change his mind at the last minute. He looked up the topmost ladder and got scared clean through.

What if I get up there and get dizzy? What if I fall? He didn't need a second guess to know what would happen to him if *that* happened.

But if he didn't start climbing, the guys would get suspicious.

He put his foot on the first rung of the

ladder and started to climb. He didn't look down . . . only up. He tried not to think of how far the ground was below him.

At last he reached the top. He went through the door into the cabin, his heart pounding wildly.

He had made it. He had climbed up the Tower for the first time. He had broken the spell.

He saw the others standing along the wall, looking out over their small town of Kellsburg.

Look at that kid Pete Nettles. You'd think he'd be scared stiff up here one hundred feet in the air. But he stands there like a veteran. Height doesn't bother him a bit.

Without his glasses, Buzz had a little difficulty picking out the various buildings he was familiar with. But far across

100

town he could see the football field and next to it the baseball field. He could see the glass factory and trucks backing up and driving away from it. It was like looking at a toy city with real-life people in it.

Then the guys began recognizing cars and, in some cases, people. They made a game out of it. Buzz tried to see what he could do, too. But without his glasses it was almost impossible for him to recognize a soul. He made guesses. Whether he was right or wrong didn't make any difference. He was having fun.

Then Pete shouted, "Hey, Corky, look!"

Pete was pointing downward and to the left of the Tower. Buzz looked. Suddenly he was overcome by a mixture of happiness and fear.

"It's Dad!" he said. "I'd better go! See you later, guys!"

He ran to the door and opened it.

"So long, Corky!" said Pete.

Frosty and Tony said "So long," too.

The first instant that Buzz looked down the ladder frightened him. He almost started to sway. He waited a moment till his head cleared, then started down. He reached bottom, then ran down the path to the street. Once he turned and waved to the boys, then ran on.

Home was a long way away. When he got tired of running he walked awhile. Then he ran again.

He burst into the house. There were Corky, Dad, Joan, and Mom in the living room . . . all looking at him. He stood there, looking back at them in silence.

He knew — he just *knew* — that it was no secret any more what he and Corky had done this afternoon.

"Put on your glasses, Buzz," said Dad seriously. "I want to make sure who I'm talking to."

Buzz's face turned fire-hot. He went to his bedroom, got the glasses, and put them on.

"That's better," Dad said. "So you played football in Corky's place, did you?"

Buzz nodded stiffly. He was looking directly at Dad, but from the corner of his eye he could see that a smile was playing on Joan's lips and on Mom's. Corky's face was as sober as a dog's.

"And you got away with it?"

Buzz nodded again.

"There was no harm done, Dad," he

said. And now that he had forced the first words out, he went on, "You know how bad Corky wanted to see that Giants-Bears game, Dad. This might be the only time in his life he'd have the chance to see two great football teams play. And the Giants are his favorites. There . . . there was no harm done, Dad. No one needs to know that it was me who played in the game today and not Corky. Not once did anyone suspect . . ."

"All right, all right," interrupted Dad. "You pulled off a great job impersonating your brother. But just because you two look alike doesn't mean that you can switch around your lives."

He got off the chair, stuffed his hands hard into his pockets, and walked over to Buzz.

Buzz was scared stiff. He wasn't sure

what was coming now. Probably a good whacking on that spot where it did the most good.

"Buzz, I wasn't too surprised when Corky confessed to me on the way home about this unbelievable switch you boys pulled," Dad said. "I'm not surprised either that you pulled if off as neatly as you did, in spite of the fact that you've hardly ever played football before. I know you're a pretty smart boy. And very clever, too. But you have let this smartness, this cleverness, get the better of you. You've twisted it to make it do wrong things. This time, by impersonating Corky on the football field, you went way out. And I mean you really went way out."

Buzz nodded. He certainly had to agree with that.

The phone rang. Joan went to answer it.

Buzz sighed. He could breathe freely for a moment.

"Corky, it's for you."

Corky went over and picked up the receiver.

"Yes, this is Corky. Who? Dougie?" He listened awhile, open-mouthed. "*I* told you that? When? Oh . . . oh!"

Buzz stared at him. Dougie Byrd! He remembered seeing Dougie at the field for a moment — that one moment he had forgotten that he wasn't Corky — and asking Dougie to come over tonight to play chess.

"Okay, Dougie," said Corky. "I'll see you after supper. 'Bye."

He hung up and stared at his brother with a dazed look.

10

"THAT was Dougie Byrd!" exclaimed Corky. "He said that *I* had asked him to come over to play a game of chess!"

"Well . . . it was me who had asked him," said Buzz sorrowfully. "I saw him at the game while I was running after a football. For a second I'd forgotten that I was supposed to be you."

"I guess you did," snapped Corky. "Well, when he comes, *you* play him. I'm not. He'd beat my pants off."

He walked into the living room and dropped unhappily into a chair.

"So what if he beats your pants off?" said Buzz. "At least you know how to play the game. Play him one game. Then just tell him that you guess you didn't get so much from those books as you thought."

Corky stared at him. "What books?"

"The books that I borrowed from the library!" Buzz stamped out of the room and returned with the books on chess. "These!" he said. "I got them so that I could learn more about the game."

"One moment, please, boys," Dad said, raising his hand. "The whole problem could be solved very simply."

Buzz and Corky turned to him as one. "How's that, Dad?" asked Buzz.

"By just telling him the truth. That it was really you and not Corky who was playing football."

"Oh, no, Dad!" cried Corky, jumping to his feet. "I can't let him know that! The whole town of Kellsburg would hear about it in no time and then I'd really be kicked off the team!"

"But the truth will have to be known sometime, Corky," said Dad.

"Maybe sometime, Dad," said Corky. "But not now. Please. And not to Dougie. Give me a break, Dad! Don't you want me to play football?"

"Okay, okay," said Dad, lifting his hands in surrender. "We won't tell Dougie. In that case, get this business straight about what Buzz told Dougie. Who did you tell him got the books, Buzz — you or Corky?"

Buzz thought a minute, then slowly explained exactly what had happened.

When it was clearly understood that

Buzz had told Dougie that it was he who had gotten the books and that Corky had read them, too, Dad said, "Now let's get back to where we were before that telephone call interrupted us." He looked at Corky. "I know you said that you might get kicked off the team, Corky, but you admitted to me in the car that what you and Buzz did wasn't right. What are you going to do about it?"

Corky and Buzz exchanged looks.

"Bob," Mom broke in, "I'm about as guilty as the boys. I could have stopped Buzz from going to the game, but I didn't. So I'm at fault, too."

Dad stared at her with disbelief. "Don't tell me you were in cahoots with the twins, Kate!"

"Not quite," she said, a faint smile on her lips. "But after you and Corky had

110

left for the game, out comes Buzz in Corky's football uniform. Honestly, I really thought he was Corky for a minute."

"And you let him —"

"I told him to get right back to his room and take that uniform off," said Mom. "Right off he started explaining to me how much seeing the pro-football game meant to Corky. And . . . very effectively, too, I tell you . . . what it would mean to Corky if he didn't show up at his football game. So . . . I gave in."

Dad still looked stunned, as Mom, smiling, prepared to set the table for supper.

Dougie arrived after supper. He and Corky started playing chess, and in just four moves Dougie had one of Corky's bishops trapped. He gave up a couple of

pawns, then came up with another spar-
kling move that took Corky's queen. He
did some maneuvering with his own
queen and rooks, and the next thing
Corky knew he was checkmated.

Dougie's freckles rolled into one as he
smiled triumphantly at Corky.

"Guess the books didn't help much,
did they, Corky?"

"Guess not," said Corky, rising from
the table. "Play Buzz. Maybe they
helped him."

Buzz and Dougie won one game
apiece, then agreed to play off the rub-
ber at some other time.

Buzz did wish, though, that Corky
would get more interested in chess. He
would really enjoy playing with him. It
wasn't fun to play against poor compe-
tition.

That night, while they lay in their beds, Buzz told Corky about going up the Tower for the first time, and about the fun he had playing football. It was, he said, the best day he'd had in his whole life.

"The Tower?" Corky said. "*You* went up the Tower?"

"That's right," said Buzz. "With Pete, Frosty, and Tony. It wasn't just playing the game, Corky, or climbing up in the Tower. It was the guys. The way they treated me, thinking that I was you. It . . . well, it's really hard to explain, Corky."

He was quiet awhile. And then he said, "Corky, would . . . would you mind if I played in your place again next week?"

11

CORKY popped his head up like a jack-in-the-box and stared across at his brother. "Are you crazy?"

"No. I'm perfectly sane, Corky. But playing in that football game today made me feel like a different person."

"Of course," said Corky. "It made you feel like me." He dropped his head back to the pillow and drew the covers up to his neck. "Go to sleep, Buzz. Tomorrow you'll feel like yourself again."

"I know," said Buzz unhappily.

How could he make Corky understand what it meant to him to be with those guys?

"I don't want to be like myself again," he said after thinking a bit. "That's what I'm trying to say, Corky. Today I found out how good it felt to have guys treat me, well . . . like a human being. Like someone they were glad to have around."

There was silence from Corky's bed for a minute. "Did Goose Marsh invite you over to his house for cookies? Boy, those raisin cookies his mother makes! I think they're even better — "

"Yes, he invited me over," said Buzz, remembering the never-to-be-forgotten moment. "I think they're horrible!"

Corky laughed. "I know. You hate raisin cookies!"

115

"Hate 'em is right."

"And Pete Nettles . . . did he say anything to you?"

"You think he didn't? He even bought me an ice cream soda! And I . . . I've always treated him like a dumb animal. That's what I mean, Corky. You have the friends because you . . . well, you treat them like human beings, not like dumb animals." A lump rose in his throat. "Oh, well, let's go to sleep, Cork."

Silence again. Buzz heard Corky's soft breathing.

Then Corky said, "Buzz, Dad and Mom wouldn't let you play in place of me. You saw how mad Dad was that you played today. He'd never let you do that again."

"I know, Corky," said Buzz. "Oh, well, forget it, Corky."

116

Beginning the next day, Buzz was a changed person. At least he tried to act changed. Every time he saw Goose Marsh, Tony Krebbs, Jimmy Briggs, Pete Nettles, or anyone else he knew, he spoke with a friendlier attitude than he had ever used before.

The boys did not act differently toward him, though. He got discouraged and almost gave up.

Heck, he thought. *They're not trying to be friendly. They're still acting like a bunch of jerks. Why should I go out of my way to try to be friendly to them?*

"You can't expect them to act different in a week," said Corky, when Buzz told him about it. "Maybe they think you're acting, or something. Maybe it would be a good idea if you joined a team, Buzz."

"I don't know about that . . . I'm not keen about football. But if I played this Sunday, too . . ."

He paused, and Corky stared at him.

"That Craig Smith, for instance," Buzz went on. "I never thought he was smart enough to captain a football team. But he called some plays last week that were the right ones at just the right time. I bet he'd make a good chess player."

"Chess!" snorted Corky. "That's all you have in that brain of yours!"

The Otters practiced on Tuesday. Buzz went along with Corky. He sat on the sideline and watched. Coach Hayes had the boys drill on blocking and tackling, then had them scrimmage. They played rough and hard. Buzz could hear the sound of their helmets and shoulder pads

118

battering each other even from where he sat.

He couldn't see any fun in that. Getting knocked around and poked in the ribs by hard helmets wasn't for him. He'd rather play something safe, like chess.

But it was on the football field that he had learned what it meant to have guys talk with you, laugh with you, and joke with you. Those fellows were the same off the field, too. Their friendship with Corky proved it.

Something happened to Alan Rogers, so Bobby Loberg took his place. Buzz saw Coach Hayes look at Alan's hand and then administer first aid to it. Alan didn't go in again. *The Otters will miss Alan badly on Sunday,* thought Buzz, *if he can't play.*

Buzz accompanied Corky to the practice sessions on Wednesday and Friday, too. There was supposed to be practice on Thursday, but it rained so hard that the coach called it off.

Then, during scrimmage on Friday, Buzz saw someone lying on the field after a play and not getting up. A chill rippled along his spine as he recognized the number on the back of the player's jersey — 76.

Corky's number!

He stood up on his feet and began chewing his fingernails nervously. Coach Hayes ran out, knelt beside Corky, and felt his ankle.

Buzz saw Corky wince.

Then the coach and Craig Smith helped Corky to his feet. They got on

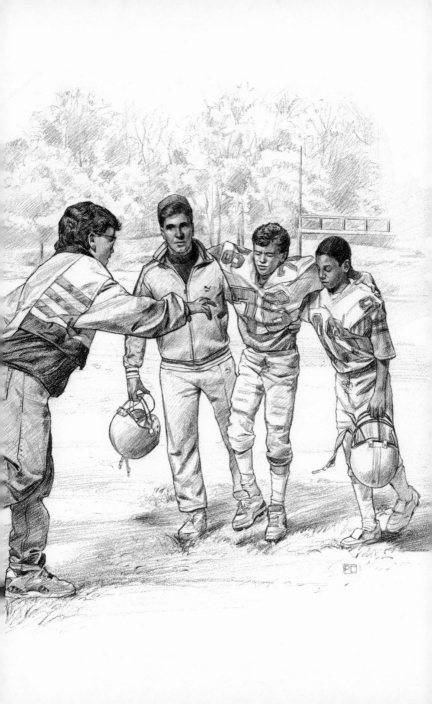

either side of him and helped him off the field.

Buzz ran over.

"Your brother sprained his ankle, Buzz," said the coach. "I'll drive him home so that he can apply a cold pack to it. This is tough luck for your brother and for the team. We play the Cougars Sunday."

12

DAD looked at Buzz long and thoughtfully.

"I know how you feel, Buzz," he said at last. "Your mother and I had quite a talk about it Sunday. Just about the same time you and Corky were talking in your bedroom."

"Then, can I, Dad?" pleaded Buzz. "Corky wouldn't play anyway. His ankle isn't completely healed. Can't I just wear his uniform and sit on the bench?"

Dad looked at Mom and Mom looked

123

at Dad as if this were really an impossible situation.

"Well . . . what do you think, Kate?" asked Dad.

"I think the boys should do exactly what we said they should."

Buzz's brows shot up. "What is that, Mom?"

"Mom and I think that you and Corky should tell Coach Hayes and the team just what you did," Dad answered. "We think it's better than trying to keep it a secret. It will bother your consciences later. And both of you — Mom and I, too — might be sorry. What do you think?"

Buzz looked unhappily at Corky. "I don't know. What do you think, Corky?"

He knew Dad and Mom were right. But if they told the coach about their switching places with each other his chance of playing in the next game would surely go down the drain.

Corky shrugged. "I think we'd better tell them," he said.

Buzz shrugged, too. "Okay. Guess we'll tell them. And guess I might as well forget about playing Sunday."

They waited until after dinner to see Coach Hayes, because they knew that he worked every Saturday morning.

The coach lived on Palmer Avenue, not far from their own street. Buzz and Corky found him in the backyard, playing football catch with Tony Krebbs, Frosty Homan, and Craig Smith.

"Well, hi, boys!" Coach Hayes smiled. "How's the ankle, Cork?"

"Not so good," replied Corky.

Buzz hadn't figured on anyone's being with the coach. He had thought that he and Corky could make their confession to Coach Hayes, and then Coach Hayes could tell the team.

His face reddened as the coach turned to him. "And how are you, Buzz?"

"I'm fine," Buzz said.

Then he looked at Corky and Corky looked at him, and Corky said: "You tell him. It was your idea in the first place."

Coach Hayes frowned. He tucked the football under his arm and came closer to them.

"Guess those three guys might as well hear this, too," Buzz said.

"Okay." The frown on the coach's face deepened. "Come here, fellas. Buzz has something to tell us."

Tony, Frosty, and Craig came forward and stood beside him.

"Just wanted to tell you that it wasn't Corky who played in that game last Sunday," Buzz confessed. "It was me."

The eyes of all four listeners opened wide.

"It was me," repeated Buzz. "Corky wanted to see the Giants-Bears game in the worst way, so I told him I'd take his place . . ."

And he went on to explain the whole thing, why he did it and everything. And Coach Hayes, and the three guys beside him, stared as if thunderstruck.

And then Coach Hayes started to laugh and couldn't stop laughing for a whole minute. Even the boys with him laughed.

"No wonder I thought it was odd that Corky was playing his tackle position so strangely at times!" he said, drying the laugh tears from his eyes. "Not once did I suspect . . . Boy! You twins certainly pulled that off slick!"

Buzz's heart was beating like an old alarm clock. "You won't kick Corky off the team because I played in his place, then, will you, Mr. Hayes?"

The coach thought a bit. "No, I won't, Buzz. Matter of fact, what are *you* doing tomorrow afternoon?"

Buzz stared. "Who? Me?"

"Yes, you," said the coach.

"N-nothing," murmured Buzz, wide-eyed.

"Then, how would you like to play in Corky's place, seeing as how he has a bad ankle and can't play anyway?"

Buzz's heart throbbed. And he had thought he wouldn't have a chance anymore!

"I sure would!" he said.

"Wait a minute." Coach Hayes turned to the three boys beside him. "I'm going to tell the rest of the team what Corky and Buzz just told us. But what's your opinion? Okay if Buzz takes Corky's place again?"

Buzz looked at them. For a moment his heart stood still.

All three boys smiled happily.

"You bet!" said Craig.

"Sure!" said Frosty.

"I'm all for it!" said Tony.

Buzz was filled with excitement. He looked at Corky and Corky looked at him. They couldn't say anything for a full half-minute.

130

13

SUNDAY was a cold, bleak day. The sky was scudded with gray clouds, the sun peeking through only occasionally.

The Cougars strutted around the field like cocky roosters. They had won their first two games, and were confident that they would beat the Otters, too.

The Otters won the toss and chose to receive. Abe West, the Cougars' husky fullback, kicked the ball. Craig caught it on his eighteen and ran it back to his twenty-eight.

Buzz watched the game from the bench. The coach had Toi Ying playing right tackle.

I wonder if he'll put me in, Buzz thought. *I just wonder.*

He wasn't wearing his glasses. The coach had said it might be dangerous to play tackle with them on. It was sure hard to see things in the distance without them. But he didn't care. He just wanted to see if the guys would really be friendly toward him now that they knew he was Buzz and not Corky.

Frosty Homan gained five yards on a run through left tackle. Then Bobby Loberg picked up another two on a run around right end. On the third down Craig flipped a screen pass to Bobby and

Bobby plowed ahead six yards for a first down. They moved the ball to the Cougars' thirty-eight-yard line, and lost it on a fumble.

With three minutes to go, Coach Hayes came over, smiled. "Okay, Buzz. Go in at the next down in place of Toi Ying."

Buzz went in. On the very first play he was off side.

"That's okay, Buzz!" said Craig, as the referee counted off five yards against the Otters. "Watch it the next time."

The Cougars had the ball on the Otters' eleven-yard line. With second down and three to go, the Cougar quarterback tried the keeper play. He didn't get anywhere. Abe West bucked. He gained two yards. Not enough for a first down.

"Thataway to go, guys!" said Craig, running behind the linemen and hitting them on their rumps. "Hold them one more time and I'll give you a medal."

On their last down, Abe West tried to buck the line again. It was close . . . so close that the referee called in the linesmen with their chain to measure.

Short by inches!

"Are we lucky!" cried Goose, smacking Buzz on the shoulder. "Let's go now, men!"

Buzz's heart warmed. Already the guys were treating him as one of their own. Boy, that smack on the shoulder sure felt good.

They gained five yards on two plays. Then a whistle blew, announcing the end of the first quarter.

The teams changed goals. The ball was put on the Otters' thirteen-yard line.

Third down, five to go. Craig called for a double-reverse. He took the snap from center, handed off to Bobby, who was running hard toward the left side. Then Bobby handed off to Jimmy, who was running toward the right side.

Buzz blocked his man as best he could. But the man pushed him aside and bolted through the line. He just missed grabbing Jimmy by the jersey.

Buzz saw Jimmy speeding around right end, gaining yardage with every step. He saw the Cougar linebackers shift from the left side of the field to the right side. The play had fooled them completely.

Buzz bolted forward. He threw himself

in front of a linebacker and the Cougar player went sprawling over him.

Buzz looked up. Jimmy was still running. The Cougar safety man was gaining ground on him fast. He was almost upon Jimmy . . .

Then Buzz saw someone running behind the speedy halfback. It was Craig Smith!

Just as the Cougar safety man started to tackle Jimmy, Jimmy lateraled the ball behind him. Craig caught it . . . and raced all the way down the field for a touchdown!

The Otter fans cheered so loudly that they must have been heard for miles around.

Frosty kicked for the extra point. The ball sailed straight between the uprights. The Otters went into the lead, 7 to 0.

The Cougars threatened to score when they succeeded in throwing a completed pass that went for thirty-five yards. They got to the Otters' five-yard line. Then their quarterback messed up their chances by fumbling a snap from center. Gary O'Brien recovered the ball for the Otters on the two-yard line!

Craig stood back in the end zone as he called signals. At the snap Buzz's man charged past him so quickly that Buzz was thrown off balance. The next instant he heard the shrill blast of the referee's whistle.

He looked around and saw Craig on the ground, tackled.

"Safety!" said the referee. "Two points!"

The half ended a few plays later. The boys stopped play and walked tiredly off the field.

As they got closer to the bleachers, Buzz saw Mom, Dad, Joan, and Corky sitting with Goose Marsh's parents. Dad was leaning forward and saying something to Mr. and Mrs. Marsh. All at once they all broke out laughing.

14

THE Cougars rolled that second half. Within three minutes their quarterback, Jack Sterns, pulled off a quarterback sneak that netted them eighteen yards. This put them on the Otters' nine-yard line.

Jack tried a pass which was knocked down by Craig. He tried another, down in the right corner, where the endline met the sideline. Jimmy missed knocking it down by inches.

The Cougar receiver caught it and

went over for a touchdown. Abe West converted and the Cougars went into the lead, 9 to 7.

The Cougars held the lead going into the fourth quarter.

Within one minute they pulled off a reverse play that went for twenty-eight yards. It was a play that made Buzz sick. The ball-carrier had zipped right past him. He hadn't been on his toes and his man had knocked him aside like a ten-pin. *Coach Hayes will take me out now for sure,* he thought.

And Coach Hayes did.

"You had your shoulders up, Buzz. Remember what I told you. Keep down. Drive forward with your shoulders. You'll be less likely to lose balance that way." He chuckled. "Might make a football player out of you yet!"

Buzz laughed.

The Cougars lost the ball on a fumble on the Otters' twenty-four-yard line. Coach Hayes sent Buzz back into the game.

In the huddle, Tony Krebbs and Frosty Homan, crouching on either side of Buzz, gave him a friendly pat on the back. Craig, straight across from him, looked him directly in the eye, then at the others around him.

"Come on, guys. Let's do something. Those Cougars aren't better than we are."

"They took out Puffy Williams," said Frosty Homan. "He was their best tackle. How about running a play through there?"

"Okay. We'll try it," said Craig. "Mike . . . Robin, open that hole!"

They broke out of the huddle, hurried to the line of scrimmage. At the snap

Craig turned, handed the ball off to Frosty, and Frosty plunged through left tackle. The hole was there and Frosty kept going. He went for nine yards.

"Good going!" said Craig.

Bobby Loberg bucked through the same place for another six yards and a first down.

"Let's try a run through our right side this time," said Craig. "Buzz . . . Pete, now it's your turn!"

"Just come along!" Buzz smiled.

Jimmy Briggs carried. He picked up only two. On the second down Craig heaved a pass to Goose. It was intercepted! Goose tackled the Cougar man almost on the spot, but the damage was done. The ball was back in the Cougars' possession.

They moved the ball across the stripes slowly, as if they weren't in a hurry at all.

But that was because the Otter defense was making it seem so.

The seconds ticked away swiftly. There were only two and half minutes left to play. Buzz saw the sweat on Craig's face. Craig, as well as the other players, wanted badly to win. But this seemed to be a battle between quarterbacks. Between Craig Smith and Jack Sterns.

"We have to get that ball," said Craig. "We have to!"

Two minutes left. The Cougars had the ball on the Otters' twenty-two. They gained three yards on a line buck. Another two on a buck.

"Hold that line, men!" shouted Craig. "Hold it!"

A screen pass! A fumble! Buzz saw the ball bouncing crazily on the ground. Saw a Cougar player rush toward it. With all

143

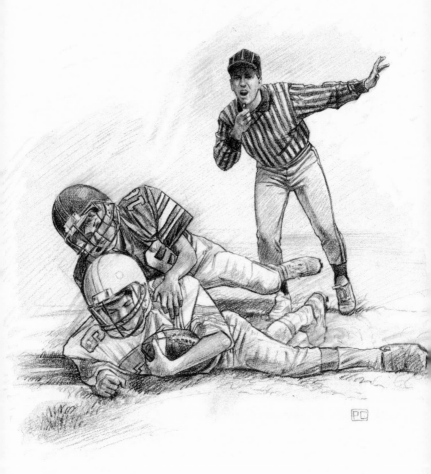

the speed he could muster he plunged after the ball . . . fell on it!

The Cougar player fell on him and tried to pull the ball out of his hands. Buzz hung on desperately. The whistle shrilled. When Buzz got up he saw the referee pointing toward the Cougars' goal!

Craig, Tony, and Mike all slapped him happily on the back. "Good going, Buzz! Now let's go! Let's move!"

The Otters moved with line plunges, short passes, reverses. Craig tried them all and they worked. And then, with forty seconds to go, he pulled the unexpected . . . the long one.

Goose was running far down the field. The pass was a beautiful spiral. Almost too far. Goose ran harder, caught it, and went over for the touchdown.

15

FROSTY missed the uprights by three feet. No one cared. A few seconds later the game was over. The Cougars had taken their first beating of the season — 13 to 9.

The Otters hugged each other, jumped, laughed, cheered.

"Hey, Buzz!" cried Goose. "My mother's baked more of those raisin cookies this weekend! Come over and bring Cork!"

146

Buzz almost made a face. Then smiled. "Maybe I will!" he answered.

A smiling figure ran across the field and flung an arm around him. "Learned any more about chess from those books, Corky?"

"Not me!" Buzz chuckled. "I'll never catch on to that game, Dougie! Chess takes brains!"

Dougie laughed. "See you later, Corky!" he said, and ran off.

I wonder where that little squirt Pete Nettles is, thought Buzz. He usually . . .

Then there was Pete, bolting across the field toward him, a mile-wide grin on his face.

"Nice game, Corky!" he cried. "I knew you guys would beat the Cougars! I'm glad you did! Boy, were they getting cocky!"

"No one's too good for us Otters," said Buzz.

"Right! See you later, Corky!"

Pete broke away from Buzz and Buzz thought: *Someday I'll have to tell him, too. And Dougie. Can't let them live their whole lives not knowing the truth.*

He headed for the bleachers, where he spotted Mom, Dad, Joan, and Corky waiting for him, broad grins on their faces.

Later that afternoon there was a knock on the door. Buzz answered it. There stood Goose Marsh, Frosty Homan, and Tony Krebbs.

"Hi, Buzz!" said Goose, smiling. "Nice game!"

Buzz grinned. "Thanks. Come on in."

They stepped inside.

149

"We're going over to the Tower," said Goose. "Do you and Corky want to come along? It *was* you who climbed the Tower with us last week, wasn't it, Buzz?"

"Right!" Buzz laughed. So did Goose and the others.

"Boy! You sure had us fooled then!" said Goose. "What are you two guys going to do next?"

"I'll tell you what we're *not* going to do," replied Buzz. "And that is switch ourselves again! Right, Corky?"

"Right, Buzz!"

The boys got their coats and caps, said, "See you later!" to Mom, Dad, and Joan, and followed Goose, Frosty, and Tony out the door.

How many of these Matt Christopher sports classics have you read?

Baseball
- ❏ Baseball Pals
- ❏ Catcher with a Glass Arm
- ❏ The Diamond Champs
- ❏ The Fox Steals Home
- ❏ The Kid Who Only Hit Homers
- ❏ Look Who's Playing First Base
- ❏ Miracle at the Plate
- ❏ No Arm in Left Field
- ❏ Shortstop from Tokyo
- ❏ The Year Mom Won the Pennant

Basketball
- ❏ Johnny Long Legs
- ❏ Long Shot for Paul

Dirt Bike Racing
- ❏ Dirt Bike Racer
- ❏ Dirt Bike Runaway

Football
- ❏ Catch That Pass!
- ❏ The Counterfeit Tackle
- ❏ Football Fugitive
- ❏ Tight End
- ❏ Touchdown for Tommy
- ❏ Tough to Tackle

Ice Hockey
- ❏ Face-Off
- ❏ Ice Magic

Soccer
- ❏ Soccer Halfback

Track
- ❏ Run, Billy, Run

All available in paperback from Little, Brown and Company

Join the Matt Christopher Fan Club!

To become an official member of the Matt Christopher Fan Club,
send a 10 x 13-inch self-addressed envelope with 75 cents postage to:

Matt Christopher Fan Club
34 Beacon Street
Boston, MA 02108